TIMELESS CLASSICS

GREAT EXPECTATIONS

Charles Dickens

– ADAPTED BY –

Joanne Suter

SADDLEBACK
EDUCATIONAL PUBLISHING

TIMELESS CLASSICS

Literature Set 1 (1719-1844)

A Christmas Carol
The Count of Monte Cristo
Frankenstein
Gulliver's Travels
The Hunchback of Notre Dame
The Last of the Mohicans

Oliver Twist
Pride and Prejudice
Robinson Crusoe
The Swiss Family Robinson
The Three Musketeers

Literature Set 2 (1845-1884)

The Adventures of Huckleberry Finn
The Adventures of Tom Sawyer
Around the World in 80 Days
Great Expectations
Jane Eyre
The Man in the Iron Mask

Moby Dick
The Prince and the Pauper
The Scarlet Letter
A Tale of Two Cities
20,000 Leagues Under the Sea

Literature Set 3 (1886-1908)

The Call of the Wild
Captains Courageous
Dracula
Dr. Jekyll and Mr. Hyde
The Hound of the Baskervilles
The Jungle Book

Kidnapped
The Red Badge of Courage
The Time Machine
Treasure Island
The War of the Worlds
White Fang

SADDLEBACK
EDUCATIONAL PUBLISHING
www.sdlback.com

ISBN-13: 978-1-61651-078-7
ISBN-10: 1-61651-078-1
eBook: 978-1-60291-812-2

Printed in the United States of America
15 14 13 12 11   1 2 3 4 5

| Contents |

| 1 |

A Convict
on the Marsh

My family name is Pirrip, and my first name is Philip. As a baby, I put both names together and called myself Pip.

I lived with my sister and her husband, the blacksmith, in the marsh country. My first clear memory is of one cold day in my seventh year. I was in the lonely churchyard visiting my parents' graves. I knew that the dark flat land past the churchyard was the marshes. I knew that the gray line was the river and that the wind came in from the sea. And I knew that the sad bundle of shivers starting to cry was Pip.

"Hold your noise!" cried a terrible voice. A man stood up among the graves. "Keep still, you little devil, or I'll cut your throat!"

The frightful man was dressed in rough gray clothes. A great iron was on his leg and a rag was wound around his head. He seized me by the chin.

"Oh! Don't cut my throat, sir!" I begged. "Pray don't do it, sir."

"Tell me your name!" growled the man. "Quick!"

"Pip, sir."

"Where do you live? Point out the place!"

I pointed to our village, a mile or more away. I tried not to cry.

"Now," said the man, "where are your mother and father?"

"Why, over there, sir!" I said, pointing to their gravestones.

"Then who do ye live with—that is if I *let* ye live?"

"My sister, sir—wife of Joe Gargery, the blacksmith."

"Blacksmith, eh?" said he, looking at the iron on his leg. Then he took down my arms and tipped me back. "Get me a file," he says. "And get me food, or I'll have your heart and liver out! Bring them to me there tomorrow morning." He pointed to a bank of earth in the distance. "Don't say a word about me—or your

heart and your liver shall be roasted and ate!"

I said I would get him the file. And I promised to get what food I could. Then I ran home without stopping.

At home the blacksmith forge was shut up. Joe was alone in the kitchen. He was a goodnatured fellow with blond hair and blue eyes. My sister, Mrs. Joe, had black hair and eyes and was tall and bony. As she so often said, she had "brought me up by hand." This meant that she often laid her heavy hand upon me—and upon Joe, too.

"Mrs. Joe is out looking for you, Pip," Joe warned me. "And she's got Tickler with her!"

I hung my head. Tickler was a piece of cane, worn smooth by raps on my frame.

"Listen! She's a-coming!" said Joe. "Get behind the door, old chap."

My sister threw the door open. Grabbing my arm, she put Tickler to work. "Where have you been, you monkey? It's hard enough for me, being the blacksmith's wife, without being a bad boy's mother!"

All evening I pictured the man on the marshes. I thought about the file and food I must soon steal.

Because it was Christmas Eve, I was put to stirring pudding for the next day. "Hark!" said I as I stirred. "Was that *guns*, Joe? What does it mean?"

"There was a convict off last night," said Joe. "They fired warning of him. Now it seems another one must have escaped."

"Who's firing?" said I.

"Guards on the prison ships!" cried my sister. She pointed her needle and thread. "Right across the marshes. People are put in those ships because they murder and rob. Now get off to bed!"

I went up to my dark room. I was in terror of my promise to the man with the iron!

At dawn, I went downstairs. Every board seemed to cry, "Stop, thief! Get up, Mrs. Joe!" I stole bread and cheese and took brandy from the stone bottle. I took a beautiful round pork pie. I got a file from Joe's toolbox. Then I ran for the marshes.

It was a damp morning. The marsh mist was thick. Before long, I saw a man sitting with his back toward me. When I touched him on the shoulder, he jumped up. It was *not* the man I had met!

This man was also dressed in rough gray clothes. He too had an iron on his leg. He swore at me and then ran into the mist. I felt my heart turn over. I dare say I should have felt a pain in my liver, too, if I had known where it was!

Then I saw the right man, limping to and fro. He grabbed the bottle of brandy and poured it down his throat. After gobbling the food, he smeared his ragged sleeve over his eyes.

I felt sorry for him then, and I made bold to say, "I am glad you enjoy the food."

"Thanks to you, my boy, I do."

"Will you leave any for him?"

"Him? Who's him?"

"The other man I saw just now, over yonder. He was dressed like you, only with a hat," I explained. "And with the same reason for needing a file."

He grabbed me by the collar and stared. "*Where is he?* Show me the way he went. I'll pull him down! Give me the file, boy!"

Then he was down on the wet grass, filing at his leg iron like a madman. I was very much afraid of him again. I told him I had to go, but he took no notice. The last I saw of him, his head was bent and he was working at the iron on his leg. The last I heard of him, the file was still rasping away.

| 2 |

The Capture

I expected someone would be waiting at home to arrest me for stealing the food. But Mrs. Joe was busy getting ready for Christmas.

"And where have *you* been?" she asked. Joe secretly crossed two fingers and showed them to me. It was our warning sign that my sister was in a cross temper.

I said I had been down at the village to hear the Christmas carols.

Mrs. Joe was fixing a fine dinner of a pickled pork leg and roast stuffed fowls. The pudding was on to boil. Clearly no discovery had been made of the missing food and file.

At half past one, I opened the door. Mr. Pumblechook, a well-to-do grain merchant in the village, had come to dine.

As we sat down to Christmas dinner, old

Pumblechook laid an eye on me. "Be grateful, boy," he said, "to them which brought you up by hand."

With that, my sister began to list the problems I had caused. Just when I felt I might get through the day, my sister stood. "You must taste," she said, "a nice pork pie."

As she went out to get it, I ran for my life. But I got no farther than the door. There I ran into a party of soldiers. They all carried muskets. One held a pair of handcuffs.

At the strange sight of soldiers on our doorstep, the dinner party rose. Mrs. Joe came back from the pantry and stared. She quickly forgot the missing pork pie.

"Excuse me," said a soldier, "but I want the blacksmith. These handcuffs are broken. Can you fix them?"

"Are you after convicts, sir?" asked Mr. Pumblechook.

"Two of them!" answered a soldier. "They're out on the marshes. Anybody here seen anything of them?"

Everybody, except me, said no. No one noticed me.

Joe put on his leather apron and took the handcuffs into the forge. Soon he began to hammer and clink, hammer and clink.

When Joe's job was done, he got his coat. He said that we should go down with the soldiers and help with the hunt.

Joe and I were told to keep to the rear. I whispered, "I hope we don't find them." And Joe whispered to me, "I'd give a shilling if they had escaped, Pip."

I rode on Joe's broad shoulders. As we moved to the marshes, I looked about. Would *my* convict see me? Would he believe that I had turned him in?

All of a sudden we stopped. On the wings of the wind and rain, there came loud shouts. The soldiers ran forward like deer, and Joe too.

"Here are both men!" panted a soldier. He pointed his gun at the bottom of a ditch. "Give up, you two!"

Water was splashing about, mud was flying, and blows were being struck. Some of the soldiers went down into the ditch. They dragged out my convict and the other one as well. Both of them were bleeding and panting and swearing loudly at each other.

"He tried to murder me!" said the other convict.

"He lies!" my convict said. "He's a liar born, and he'll die a liar."

"Enough of this!" one soldier ordered. "Light those torches."

Then my convict looked round him and saw me. I shook my head, hoping to show that I had not turned him in. He gave me a look that I did not understand. But I knew I would remember his face ever after.

My convict never looked at me, except that once. He turned to the soldiers. "I wish to say something. I took some food from the blacksmith's, over yonder." My convict then turned his eyes on Joe. "Are you the blacksmith?" he said. "I'm sorry to say, I've eaten your pie."

"God knows you're welcome to it," said Joe. "We don't know what you have done, but we wouldn't have you starved to death, poor fellow. Would we, Pip?"

We followed the soldiers and their prisoners to the landing. We saw the black prison ship lying offshore like a wicked Noah's ark. We saw the two convicts rowed out and taken up the side and disappear. Then the torches were flung hissing into the water.

I never told a single living soul about my convict. I loved Joe, and the fear of losing his trust tied my tongue. First I had been afraid to avoid doing wrong. Now I was afraid to do what I knew to be right.

* * * *

When I was old enough, I was to work with Joe in the forge. Until that time, I did odd jobs. Any money I earned went into a box on the kitchen shelf.

A village school for children met each evening. It was run by an older lady who napped through most classes. With the help of a girl named Biddy, the lady also kept a little store. Biddy was an orphan, like myself. Her hair always wanted brushing, and her shoes always wanted mending. With Biddy's help I learned the alphabet.

One night, sitting in the kitchen with my slate, I wrote a note to Joe. I think this was a year after our hunt upon the marshes. I worked an hour to print this message:

mI deEr JO i opE U r KrWitE wEll
piP

Joe looked at the note with pride. "I say, Pip, old chap! What a scholar you are! Why, here's a *J*. And a *O*. *J-O, Joe!* Why don't you take me in hand, Pip, and teach *me* to read? But Mrs. Joe mustn't see what we're up to. Oh, no, she would not be happy about my being a scholar!"

Mrs. Joe had gone to market with Uncle Pumblechook that day. Joe made the fire and swept the hearth. Then we waited for the carriage. It was a dry, cold night.

"Here comes the mare," said Joe, "ringing like a peal of bells!"

Mrs. Joe and Mr. Pumblechook rushed into the warm little house.

"Now," Mrs. Joe cried out, "if this boy ain't grateful this night, he never will be! Miss Havisham wants him to go and play there. So of course he's going—and he had *better* play there!" My sister frowned at me.

I had heard of old Miss Havisham. *Everybody* had heard of Miss Havisham. She was a grim old rich lady who lived in a big gloomy house. She never came out.

"I wonder how she comes to know of our Pip!" said Joe, surprised.

"Whoever said she *knew* him?" cried my sister. "Uncle Pumblechook rents his office from her. She asked if he knew a boy. Indeed, he knows that *this* boy's fortune may be made by his going to Miss Havisham's. He will take Pip to town tonight and to Miss Havisham's in the morning."

With that, she pounced on me like an eagle on a lamb. My head was put under water. I was soaped and toweled. Then I was put into a tight, stiff suit and handed over to Uncle Pumblechook.

"Goodbye Joe," I cried out sadly.

"Goodbye, Pip, old chap!"

I had never parted from Joe before. The stars twinkled above the carriage, but they could not throw any light on my questions. Why on earth was I going to play at Miss Havisham's? And what on earth was I supposed to play at?

| 3 |

Miss Havisham
and Estella

At ten o'clock the next morning, Mr. Pumblechook and I stood outside Miss Havisham's gate. Her house was of old, dark brick. The windows had rusty bars. After ringing a bell, we waited.

A pretty young lady came across the courtyard. "So this is Pip, is it?" she said in a proud voice. "Come in, Pip."

"Come along, boy," she said. Though she called me "boy," I saw that she was about my age. She was beautiful. We went up some dark stairs. At last we came to a door. "Go in," she said. Then she walked away.

I was half afraid. I knocked and a voice from within told me to enter.

I found myself in a room lighted with candles. I saw a draped table with a gold framed looking glass. It seemed to be a fine lady's dressing table. In an armchair sat the strangest looking lady I have ever seen.

She was dressed in rich lace and silks that were all of white. She wore a long white veil. There were wedding flowers in her white hair. Bright jewels sparkled on the dressing table. Half-packed trunks lay all about. She had not quite finished dressing, for she had but one shoe on.

But everything that should have been white was faded and yellow. And the bride within the wedding gown had grown old and wrinkled. The dress hung loose upon a figure that was now skin and bone.

"Who is it?" said the lady at the table.

"It's Pip, ma'am—Mr. Pumblechook's boy. I'm here to play."

"Come close. Let me look at you."

It was then I saw that her watch had stopped at exactly 8:40. A clock in the room had stopped at the same time.

"Look at me," said Miss Havisham. "Are you afraid of a woman who has not seen the sun since you were born?"

"No," I lied.

She laid her hands upon her chest. "Do you know what I touch here?"

"Your heart?" I asked.

"Yes—and it's *broken*!" she said with a strange smile. "Now, I want to see some play. Go to the door. Call Estella!"

I called. The proud young lady came along the dark hall.

Miss Havisham called her close. She took a jewel from the table and held it against the girl's pretty brown hair. "Yours, one day, my dear. And you will use it well. Let me see you play cards with this boy."

"With *this* boy? Why, he is nothing but a common working boy!"

I thought I heard Miss Havisham whisper, "Well? You can break his heart."

Miss Havisham watched as we played.

"What coarse hands he has!" said Estella. "And what thick, ugly boots!"

I played the game to its end. Estella easily won. Then she threw down the cards.

"Go now, Pip," Miss Havisham said. "You shall come here again after six days. Estella, take the boy downstairs and give him a bite of something to eat."

I followed Estella down the stairs.

"You wait here, you boy," she said.

While I was alone, I looked at my coarse hands and my common boots. They had never troubled me before, but they did now.

Estella came back with some bread and meat. She put the food on the stones of the courtyard as if I were a dog. I was so hurt and angry that tears started to my eyes. The girl looked at my tears with delight. This gave me the power to hold them back.

"Why don't you cry?" Estella asked.

"Because I don't want to."

"You're almost crying now," she laughed. Then she pushed me outside the gate.

When Estella had gone, I leaned on a wall and cried. I kicked the wall, so bitter were my feelings. Then I set off on the four-mile walk to our forge. As I walked, I thought about being a common working boy. I thought about my coarse hands and boots.

My sister wanted to know all about Miss Havisham. I felt it would be somehow wrong to describe her as she was. So I made up tales. I said Miss Havisham was tall and dark. I said she sat in a black velvet coach. I said Miss Estella, her niece, served her cake and wine on a gold plate.

But I couldn't lie to Joe. Later, I followed him into the forge.

"Remember all that I said about Miss Havisham, Joe? It's lies."

I told him about the beautiful young lady who had called me common. I said that I wished my boots weren't so thick nor my hands so coarse.

"Are you angry with me, Joe?"

"No, old chap. But don't never tell lies no more."

When I got to my little room and said my prayers, I thought how common Estella would consider Joe. I fell asleep recalling everything that had happened at Miss Havisham's.

That day made great changes in me. But it is the same with any life. Stop a moment, you who read this. Take one day out of your life. Then think how different your path would have been without that day.

| 4 |
Two Shillings
and a Kiss

One day I awoke with an idea. I knew how I could make myself less common.

At school that evening I told Biddy I wanted to get on in life. I asked her to teach me all that she knew. Biddy agreed and I started working harder than ever.

Joe liked to smoke his pipe at a village bar called the Three Jolly Bargemen. I was to call for him there on my way home. I found Joe smoking his pipe with a man I didn't know. The stranger looked hard at me.

"What is it you call him?" he asked Joe.

"Pip," Joe answered.

"Is he a son of yours?"

Joe told how I had come to live with him. He said that I would work with him in the forge one day.

As the stranger looked at me, he stirred his drink. I alone saw he stirred it with a *file* instead of a spoon. I knew it was Joe's file—the one I had given to my convict. It was plain that this stranger knew who I was, and he knew my convict, too!

Joe got up to go. He took me by the hand.

"Stop half a moment, Mr. Gargery," said the strange man. "I think I've got a bright shilling in my pocket. If I have, the boy shall have it."

He folded the shilling in some paper. "Yours!" he said to me. "Yours, alone."

I thanked him and held tight to Joe. On the way home I could think of nothing but this odd meeting.

Of course, my sister took the shilling. It put her in a good temper. Then she looked at the paper it was wrapped in. "Two one-pound notes!" she cried out happily.

This was a great sum! My sister put them in a teapot in the parlor.

I had bad dreams that night. I saw the file coming at me, but I could not see who held it. I screamed myself awake.

The day came for me to go back to Miss

Havisham's. Estella let me in when I rang. She took me to a room on the ground floor. There were others there, too. "Stand there, boy, until you are wanted," Estella said.

The people in the room looked at me. They all called each other "Cousin" but did not seem to like each other very much. They spoke badly about a Cousin Matthew Pocket, who was not present.

When Estella returned, they stopped talking and stared.

"Now, boy!" Estella said.

I followed her along the dark hall. Then all of a sudden she stopped. She turned round and put her face quite close to mine.

"Well?" she said. "Am I pretty?"

"I think you are very pretty," I said, almost falling over her.

Then she slapped my face. "*Now* what do you think?"

"I shall not tell you."

"Why don't you cry, you coarse boy?"

"Because I'll never cry for you again," said I. This was as big a lie as was ever told. I was silently crying for her right then.

We turned to go upstairs. As we were going up, we met a gentleman coming down. He was a big man with a large, bald head and bushy black eyebrows. There were black dots where his whiskers would have been if he had not shaved them away.

"Why are you here?" he asked.

"Miss Havisham sent for me, sir," I explained.

"Well, see that you behave yourself."

Estella soon left me standing at Miss Havisham's door. I entered, and Miss Havisham motioned for me to follow her. She leaned on a stick as she walked, and she looked like a witch. We crossed the landing and entered a dark, stuffy room. Everything in it was thick with dust. In its center was a long table. A tall object sat on the table. At one time, it must have been a wedding cake. Now it was hung with cobwebs. I saw speckled spiders running in and out of it. I heard mice, too, rattling over the floor.

"Today is my birthday, Pip," said Miss Havisham. Then she had me walk her round about the table. Her hand twitched on my

shoulder. Estella entered and watched us.

"Now let me see you two play at cards!" Miss Havisham said.

Again, we played cards. Again, Estella beat me soundly and treated me rudely. This time I found my own way out.

To my surprise, I met a pale, young fellow near the gate.

"Who let you in?" he said.

"Miss Estella."

"Come and fight," said he. As if to give me reason for a fight, he dipped his head and butted it right into my stomach.

I hit out at him. He looked to be my age but was much taller, and I was a bit afraid. He danced about as if he knew how to fight. I let out another blow and bloodied his nose. Then he got to his feet and said, "Good afternoon."

At the gate, Miss Estella waited to let me out. "Come here," she said. "You may kiss me if you like."

I kissed her cheek as she turned it to me. But I felt that the kiss was given like a coin to a common boy. It meant nothing.

No mention was ever made of the pale young man or of our fight. Estella never again told me I might kiss her. On some of my visits she was friendly. At other times she would tell me she hated me.

"Does she not grow prettier?" Miss Havisham would often ask me. Then she would softly whisper to Estella, "Break their hearts. Break their hearts!"

At home, my sister waited for Miss Havisham to give me money, but none was offered.

| 5 |

A Young Man of Great Expectations

One day Miss Havisham looked closely at me. "You are growing tall, Pip!" she said. "What is the name of that blacksmith of yours?"

"Joe Gargery, ma'am."

"The time has come for you to work as his apprentice. Bring him here."

The next day Joe dressed in his best clothes. He closed up the forge, and we set off for Miss Havisham's. We left my sister in a bad temper, angry that she had not been asked to visit.

Estella showed us in. We found Miss Havisham at her dressing table. Dear old Joe sat silent. With his hair combed up like feathers, he looked like some strange bird.

Miss Havisham held out a bag. "Pip has earned this by coming here," she said.

The bag held 25 pounds! It was given over with two orders. I was now to become Joe's apprentice in the forge. And, I was told to expect no more favors.

"Am I to come here again?" I asked.

"No. Gargery is your master now," Miss Havisham answered. Mrs. Joe was thrilled with the 25 pounds. She said we must have a dinner at the Blue Boar Inn. I did not enjoy the party. I had once liked the idea of becoming a blacksmith, but not now.

I never breathed a word of these feelings to Joe. I worked hard as his apprentice. But I was always worried that Estella would see my dirty face through the window of the forge.

Joe had a second helper at the forge. He was a large, sour fellow named Orlick. I had been afraid of him since I was a child. He never seemed to like me, or Mrs. Joe either. When I became Joe's apprentice, Orlick liked me even less.

One morning when I asked Joe for a half-day off, Orlick flew into a rage. I wanted to visit Miss Havisham one more time. I claimed it was to thank her for all she'd done for me. Both

Joe and I knew I really hoped for a glimpse of Estella. In the end, Joe gave me a holiday. To keep the moody fellow happy, he gave Orlick a holiday, too.

"I came to say I am doing well as an apprentice," I told Miss Havisham.

"Ha! I see you looking for her!" Miss Havisham cried. "You are looking round for Estella! She's at school across the sea. And she's prettier than ever—loved by all!"

Her words had a wicked, gleeful ring. Then she sent me away. "Come now and then, Pip. Come on your birthday."

I headed home more unhappy about my trade and my life than ever before.

A heavy mist hung in the air. Around a bend in the road, I met Orlick. "Do you hear them?" Orlick growled at me. "The guns are firing from the prison ships. Some birds have flown their cages!"

Just then Mr. Pumblechook came running toward us. "There's something wrong," said he, "up at your place, Pip. Convicts broke into the house when Joe was out!"

I ran straight home. Our kitchen was full of

people. There was a doctor there, and there was Joe. Then I saw my sister, lying on the floor. She had been knocked out by a blow on the back of the head.

On the ground beside her lay a convict's leg iron. Right away, I believed it to be *my* convict's iron. But I did not think it was he who had struck down Mrs. Joe. I believed that one of two persons must have gotten hold of the iron and used it. It had to be either Orlick or the strange man who had shown me the file.

My sister lived. In fact, her temper improved. But now her hearing was bad and so was her memory. She never spoke a word again. She kept a slate close by and tried to write us messages.

Biddy came to live with us. She helped me and Joe take care of my sister. What a blessing Biddy was to us!

One day I opened my heart to Biddy. I told her of my love for Estella. "Oh, Biddy, if only I could fall in love with *you* instead. That would be the thing for me!"

"Ah, but you never will, you see," said

Biddy, sadly. And I knew she was right.

Time passed, and I was now in my fourth year as Joe's apprentice. It was a Saturday night. A group of us were sitting round the fire at the Three Jolly Bargemen.

I saw a gentleman watching us. "Is one of you fellows Joe Gargery, the blacksmith?" he asked.

"I am," said Joe.

"You have an apprentice, known as Pip. Is he here?"

"I am here!" I cried. I had seen this stranger on Miss Havisham's stairs.

"My name," he said, "is Jaggers. I am a lawyer in London." He turned to Joe. "I should like to talk to you and Pip alone."

Everyone stared as we left the Three Jolly Bargemen. Silently, we turned toward home. When we were alone, Jaggers spoke. "I am the lawyer for a person whose name I cannot give," he said. "This certain person has set aside a great deal of money for Pip. The boy is to go to London. He will be brought up as a gentleman. Pip shall become a young fellow of great expectations."

This was my dream! I was sure Miss Havisham was the person of whom Mr. Jaggers spoke. Miss Havisham was going to make my fortune!

To make up for his loss of an apprentice, Mr. Jaggers offered Joe money. But Joe would take nothing.

"Pip," Mr. Jaggers said, "you must agree to two things. You must never ask your benefactor's name. It will be told to you in time. Also, you must keep the name of Pip."

As I nodded, Jaggers counted out some coins. "You will need new clothes for your trip to London. When you arrive, you will be placed under a proper tutor, Mr. Matthew Pocket. In one week, take a coach to London and meet me at my office."

With that, Jaggers handed me his card and walked away.

That night Joe told Biddy my news. "Pip's to be a gentleman of fortune," he said. "And God bless him in it!"

Biddy dropped her work. She looked at me. They said they were glad for me, but there was sadness in their voices.

When my new clothes were ready, I picked them up from the tailor. I was set to leave our village at five in the morning. I told Joe that I wished to walk to the coach alone. Saying goodbye would be too sad. But I knew the truth. Now that I wore fine clothes, I did not want to walk beside Joe in his plain ones.

That last morning at home I hurried through breakfast. "I suppose I must be off!" I said. Then I kissed my sister, who was nodding in her chair. I kissed Biddy and threw my arms around Joe's neck. The last I saw of them, dear old Joe was waving his arm above his head. Biddy was wiping her eyes with her apron.

I walked a while. Then I stopped and, with one huge sob, broke into tears. I thought of going back and having a better parting. But I got on the coach instead. The mists had risen and the day was clear. The world lay spread out before me.

This is the end of the first stage of Pip's expectations.

| 6 |

London

It was midday when the horses pulled my stagecoach into the city. I must admit that London frightened me a bit. Its streets seemed rather ugly, crooked, and dirty.

I soon found Mr. Jaggers' offices. A number of people were waiting at his door.

"Mr. Jaggers is in court at present," said a clerk at a desk. "If you are Mr. Pip, you are to wait inside."

The clerk showed me to an inner office. There were piles of papers all about and another crowd of people outside. I could see that Mr. Jaggers was a busy man.

At length my guardian arrived. After a bite of sandwich and a nip of sherry, he got down to business. He quickly told me that I was to go to Barnard's Inn. There I would stay with a man called Mr. Pocket. I was to remain with young Mr. Pocket until Monday. Then I was to go with him to meet his father, who would be my teacher.

I would, Mr. Jaggers explained, get a generous allowance. I would also have credit in many shops. Mr. Jaggers said that he himself would check on my bills and pull me up if I spent too much.

"My clerk Wemmick will walk round with you to Barnard's Inn," he said.

Soon Wemmick and I were at Barnard's Inn, a shabby place in a lonely square. It was not what I had thought to find on the first day of my great expectations.

Wemmick led me up some broken stairs. On the top floor, we stopped before a chamber. MR. POCKET, JUN. was painted on the door. A note said "Return shortly."

"We shall likely meet again," Mr. Wemmick said. "Good day."

I waited for half an hour, amusing myself by writing my name in the dust. At last, I saw someone on the stairs.

"Mr. Pocket?" said I.

"Dear me!" said Mr. Pocket, Junior. "Mr.

Pip? I am so sorry to have made you wait. Pray come in."

He showed me into the two dusty rooms. I looked at him closely. He looked at me. I saw that he knew me, just as I knew him. Then he said, smiling, "Bless me, you're the boy at Miss Havisham's!"

"And you," said I, "are the pale young gentleman who started a fight!"

We both burst out laughing. He reached out his hand and said, "I hope you'll forgive me for having knocked you about so."

I saw that Mr. Herbert Pocket (for Herbert was his name), was a bit mixed up. But I did not remind him that *I* had won the fight. Instead, I politely shook hands.

"I understand you've come into good fortune," said Herbert. "Did you know that Miss Havisham had sent for *me* before you came? But she didn't take a fancy to me. Bad taste, but a fact," he laughed. "No matter. I didn't care much for her."

"For Miss Havisham?"

"For Estella. That girl is hard and stuck up. Of course, she was brought up by Miss

Havisham to get revenge on all men."

"Tell me, what relation is she to Miss Havisham?" I asked.

"Why, *none*," said he. "Only adopted."

"But why should Estella get revenge on all men? Revenge for *what*?"

"Dear me, Mr. Pip. Don't you know?" And Herbert Pocket began his tale.

"Miss Havisham's father was a rich man. He spoiled his little daughter terribly. When his wife died, he married again—they say it was to his cook. He had a second child, a son he named Arthur. Then the second wife died, and Arthur turned out rather badly. When Mr. Havisham left his fortune to his daughter, Arthur was angry. And now I come to the cruel part of the story.

"Arthur found a man to go after Miss Havisham and win her trust. She gave this man not only her heart, but great sums of money. She made plans to marry him. My father, Matthew, warned her that the fellow was no gentleman. But she was in love. She ordered my father out of the house. He has never seen her since. The wedding day came, but not the bridegroom. He wrote a letter…"

I broke in. "Did it arrive just as she was dressing for her wedding? Was it twenty minutes to nine?"

Herbert nodded. "At which moment she stopped all the clocks. The wedding never took place. Miss Havisham kept everything just as you have seen it. She has never since looked upon the light of day."

"What became of the bridegroom?" I asked. "What of Miss Havisham's brother? Are they alive now?"

Herbert shook his head. "I've told you all I know about the matter. But enough of this gloomy talk! Tomorrow we go to dinner at my father's house. If you are to be a gentleman of good fortune, we must work on your manners." Herbert said it so frankly that I did not mind. He had an open, easy way about him. I liked it very much.

As we dined, I listened to his advice. "In London, dear Pip," he began, "one does not put the knife in one's mouth. That place is reserved for the fork."

I asked Herbert what he did for a living.

He said something about insuring ships. I imagined great riches and wondered why he lived in such a shabby place. I asked him what ships he insured.

"Well," he replied, "I haven't *exactly* begun insuring yet. I am at the present looking about for the right opportunity."

It was clear that Herbert Pocket had little money and only the simplest of things. Yet his imaginary good fortune made him cheerful. I liked him for that. We got along wonderfully.

| 7 |

Dinner Parties
and a Visit from Joe

On Monday morning, I dined with Herbert at his father's house. I found Matthew Pocket to be a young-looking man in spite of his rather messy gray hair. He greeted me with a puzzled expression—one I learned that he always wore.

Mr. Pocket was a fine teacher, but did not earn much at this work. To pay the bills, he rented rooms to two students—Drummle and Startop. Bentley Drummle was a heavy, odd-looking young man. He came, I was told, from a very rich family. His parents knew that their son was a blockhead. So they had sent him to Mr. Pocket for schooling. I took a strong dislike to Drummle from the moment we met. I took much more kindly to Startop, who was a pleasure to be with.

I made up my mind to see as little as possible of Drummle. But that was not to be.

As it happened, my guardian soon sent me a dinner invitation. He asked that I bring three friends, namely Herbert Pocket, Startop, and Drummle.

I was surprised when Jaggers seemed to take a special interest in loud, sulky Drummle. "What is that fellow's name?" he asked me before dinner. "The blotchy one that looks like a spider?"

Dinner was served by a housekeeper, a big woman whom Jaggers called Molly. She was about 40, tall, and pale. She had streaming blond hair and large, faded eyes. Somehow I felt I had seen those eyes before.

As Molly cleared the table, my guardian grabbed her big hand. "If you talk of strength," he said, "I'll show you a wrist!"

Molly tried to pull away, but Jaggers held tight. "Molly, let them see your wrist."

She held out a wrist that was deeply scarred, across and across.

"There's real power in this hand," said Jaggers. "Few men are as strong. All right, Molly. You may go.

"It grows late, gentlemen," Jaggers went on.

43

"We must break up." He raised a glass. "Mr. Drummle, I drink to you."

On the walk home, Drummle was flushed with pleasure at Jaggers' attentions. The silly chap would not even walk on the same side of the street as the rest of us.

I now spent my days becoming a gentleman. This meant spending great sums of money. Whenever I needed more, I went to Mr. Jaggers. I bought fine furniture and clothing. I even hired a serving boy, although there was little for him to do.

It was on a Monday that I received a letter from Biddy. Joe was coming to London! His visit was to be the next day. Let me confess, I was not happy. I did not mind that Herbert, whom I greatly respected, might meet Joe. What strangely bothered me was that Drummle, whom I hated, would see my plain, common friend.

Early Tuesday morning I heard heavy boots on the stairs. My serving boy announced, "Mr. Gargery!"

"Joe! How are you, Joe?" I said.

With his good, honest face glowing, he

caught both my hands. He shook them up and down.

"My, you have growed!" said Joe, pumping my hands again.

I asked about my sister and Biddy. Joe said all was well. Biddy, it seemed, was teaching him to read and write. But as our visit went on, Joe seemed more and more uncomfortable. He began to call me "sir." This made me feel angry and out of temper. I had neither the good sense nor the good feeling to know that this was all my fault. If I had been easier with Joe, Joe would have been easier with me.

At last he stood. "Well, sir," he said, "I have one message to give you before I leave. It comes from Miss Havisham."

"Miss Havisham, Joe?"

"She wishes to speak to you, sir. She says that Estella has come home and would be pleased to see you."

I felt my face turn red.

"And, sir—I wish you ever well and greater fortune."

"But are you going, Joe? Surely you are coming back to dinner?"

"No, I am not," said Joe.

Our eyes met. All the "sir" melted away as he took my hand. "Pip, I feel silly in this suit. I'm wrong out of the forge and off the marshes. You won't find half so much fault if you think of me with my hammer in my hand. So bless you, old chap. Bless you!"

He went out. After a moment I hurried after him. I looked for him in the streets. But he was gone.

The next day I returned to the village. I felt I should stay at Joe's. But I stayed at the Blue Boar instead. I did not visit Joe.

I went straight to Miss Havisham's where I was greeted by a new gatekeeper. It was the last man I expected to see in that place!

"Orlick! Have you left the forge?"

"Do this look like a forge?" growled Orlick with a scowl.

I went up the dark stairs. I knocked in my old way and entered Miss Havisham's room.

She was wearing the same yellowed dress. Sitting near her was an elegant lady. The lady looked at me, and I saw Estella's eyes. I hardly knew her! She was so much changed,

so much more beautiful! I felt like the coarse and common boy again.

"Do you find her changed, Pip?" asked Miss Havisham with a mean, greedy look.

"And Estella, is *he* changed?" Miss Havisham asked her.

Estella looked at me. "Very much," she laughed. She treated me like a boy still. Yet, strangely, she lured me on.

When we were sent into the garden, Estella moved close. "You must not love me, Pip," she said. "I have no heart at all. Oh, I have a heart to be stabbed in or shot in. If it stopped beating, I would die. But you know what I mean. I have no softness there. If we are to be thrown together, you must know that I have no tenderness—none!"

We returned to the house, and I went alone to Miss Havisham's room. She drew an arm around my neck and whispered, "Love her, love her! Hear me, Pip! I raised her to be loved. I made her into what she is." Her voice rose into a wild cry. "Real love means giving up your whole heart and soul ... as I did!"

As I lay in my bed at the Blue Boar, I thought of Joe. I should have gone to see him! Tears sprang to my eyes. Then I thought of Estella—who would surely find him coarse and common. My tears soon dried. God forgive me, they soon dried.

| 8 |

Coming of Age

When I returned to London, I sent a codfish and a barrel of oysters to Joe. I hoped the gift would ease my guilt over not visiting. Then I went straight to Bernard's Inn and my friend.

"Ah, my dear Herbert," I said, "I have something to tell you!" I laid my hand on his knee. "Herbert, I love—no, I *adore*—Estella. I saw her yesterday. If I adored her before, I now doubly adore her."

"Lucky for you, then," said Herbert, "that you are picked out for her. Have you any idea of Estella's views on the subject?"

I shook my head gloomily.

"Pip, you are a fine fellow. But I have something to say that you may not like. It is about Estella. Think of the way she has been raised. Think of Miss Havisham. This may lead to miserable things in the future."

"I know it, Herbert," said I. "But I can't help it!"

"Well, now!" Herbert said, "I shall speak of happier things. You must keep this a secret. I am engaged!"

"May I ask her name?" I said.

"Clara," Herbert answered. "She lives with her sick father. On my visits I hear him upstairs, roaring and pounding the floor. The moment I begin to make money, I shall marry Clara. But," he added sadly, "a chap can't marry while he is looking about."

Herbert's announcement was followed by even greater news. I received a note by post. It had no beginning, such as *Dear Pip*, or *Dear Sir*, or *Dear Anything*. It ran thus:

I am to come to London the day after tomorrow. I will arrive by the midday coach. I believe it is settled that you should meet me. —Yours, Estella.

I could not eat. I knew no peace until I saw her face in the coach window. Wearing a fur-trimmed traveling dress, Estella was more beautiful than ever.

"I am going to Richmond," she told me.

"You are to take me. I shall live with a lady who knows the finest people."

I told her Richmond was not far, and that I hoped to see her.

"Oh, yes. You are to see me," she said. Her voice sounded tired. "It is a part of Miss Havisham's plan for me, Pip."

We took a carriage to Richmond. I stood looking at the house after Estella was inside. I thought how happy I should be if I lived there with her. Yet I knew that I had never been happy with her, but always miserable.

Meanwhile, I had grown used to spending great sums of money. Herbert had picked up my habits and was deeply in debt. We tried to tell ourselves we were having a grand time. But we were always worried. I offered to help Herbert pay off his debts. But he was too proud to accept my money.

One night we were looking over our bills when a letter dropped through the slot. "It's for you," said Herbert. He took up an envelope with a black seal. "I hope this is not bad news."

The letter told me that Mrs. J. Gargery had departed this life. Her funeral would be held on Monday. I thought of my sister sitting by the fire. I could not recall her with much tenderness. But I felt sad.

I went to the forge early Monday morning. That afternoon, my sister was laid to rest near the graves of my parents.

Biddy, Joe, and I had a cold dinner together. Joe was careful what he did with his knife and fork. He was pleased when I asked if I could sleep in my little room. I said I would be back to visit soon and often. I was hurt, I must say, to see the doubtful look on Biddy's face.

"Never too soon," said Joe. "And never too often, Pip!"

Next morning, I returned to London. There Herbert and I continued to build up our debts.

The day before my 21st birthday, a note came from Jaggers. He asked me to call upon him the next day.

I was sure the meeting concerned my coming of age. "Am I to learn today who to thank for my fortune?" I asked him.

"No, you are here for another matter, Mr. Pip. You are deeply in debt. Here is a bank note," he said, "for 500 pounds."

It was a handsome sum of money!

"At this rate each year—and at no more—you are to live. You will now take your affairs into your own hands."

As I left the inner office, I was struck with an idea. I stopped at Wemmick's desk. With the help of the clerk, I set up a plan. I would use half of my 500 pounds to give Herbert a start in business. And it would be done secretly!

One day soon after, Herbert came home grinning. He told me that an opening had come up for him at last. Seeing his happy face, I had a hard time keeping back my own tears of joy. At last my expectations had done somebody some good.

Twenty-four hours a day I thought of having Estella with me unto death. I was shocked and miserable to learn that she was keeping company with that clumsy booby, Bentley Drummle.

I had once pointed him out to her. "Look at that fellow in the corner," I said. "He has been hovering about you all night."

Estella glanced toward him. "Moths and all sorts of ugly creatures hover about a candle.

Can the candle help it?"

"But Estella, why do you encourage a man so disliked as Drummle? You know he is a stupid fellow. The only good thing he has is money. Yet I see you give him smiles such as you never give to me."

"Do you want me to trick and entrap you?"

"Do you trick and entrap *him*, Estella?"

"Yes, and many others—all but you. Now I'll say no more."

So much for the subject of heartache. I move on now to a time when an even greater blow was struck. In one instant, the roof of my life dropped down on me.

| 9 |

The Visitor

I was now 23 years of age. Not another word had I heard as to who was behind my expectations. Business had taken Herbert out of London, and I was alone in our quarters. It was a stormy night. The wind shook the house and blew out the flame in the street lamps. The clock struck 11 just as I heard footsteps on the stairs.

"Is someone there?" I called out.

"Yes," said a voice from below.

"What floor do you want?"

"The top. I'm looking for Mr. Pip."

"That is my name." I held my lamp over the stair rail. A man's face came within its light. The stranger wore a seaman's rough dress. He had long, iron-gray hair. His age seemed to be about 60. As he climbed the last stair, he held out both hands to me.

He looked about my room with an air of pleasure. It was as if he had some stake in what he saw there. When he pulled off his hat, I saw that the top of his head was bald. The long iron-gray hair grew only on the sides of his head. I did not recognize his face.

Taking a handkerchief from his pocket, he tied it around his head. Then I knew him! I saw in my mind the churchyard where we had first stood face to face!

He held out his hands. Though I did not want to, I gave him mine.

"Noble Pip!" he said. "I have never forgot your kind act."

Then he moved as if to hug me.

"You must understand!" I stopped him. "We can never be friends."

I saw with surprise that his eyes filled with tears. "I did not mean to speak harshly," said I. "I wish you a good life."

"I have been living well," my convict said. "I've been a stock breeder of sheep many, many miles across the sea." He looked around my room again. "May I make so bold," he asked with a smile, "as to ask *you* something.

How have you done so well since you was out on them marshes?"

I told him that I had been chosen to receive some property.

"Might I ask *whose* property?" he said.

"I-I don't know."

"Could I make a guess at your yearly income since you came of age?" said the convict. "Could it be 500 pounds?"

My heart beat like a hammer. I stared at him. I could scarcely breathe.

"There must have been a guardian," he said, "until you came of age. Would the first letter of that person's name be *J*?"

The truth flashed upon me in a jolt of disappointment and disgrace. I gasped for breath. The room began to spin. He caught me and helped me to the sofa. Then he knelt on one knee before me.

"Yes, Pip, my dear boy, I've made a gentleman of you. It's *me* what has done it! I swore if I ever got rich, *you* should get rich. I lived a hard life so that you should live an easy one. I worked so that you should be above work. Why, I'm your second father! Tell me—did

you ever think it might be me, Pip?"

"Oh, no, no," I answered. "Never!"

"Well, you see, it *was* me. Never a soul in on it but my own self and Mr. Jaggers!"

Oh, that he had never come! If only he had left me at the forge.

The convict talked on. He told me he had been sent to Australia as a prisoner. It was there he had made his fortune. "But it's death for me to be here," he said. "If the law finds me in England, I will be hanged."

Then he laid his hand on my shoulder.

I shuddered at the thought that his hand might be stained with blood.

"Where will you put me?" he asked. "I must sleep somewhere."

"My friend is away," I said. "You can have his room." I shuddered again. This wretched man had loaded me with his wretched gold. Now I was to have his very life in my keeping.

He went to his room, and I closed the shutters tight. Then I sat down, stunned. I fully saw how ruined I was. Miss Havisham's intentions toward me were all a dream. Estella was not meant for me. Then the greatest pain came: I realized that it was for this convict that I had turned my back on Joe.

In every rush of wind and rain, I heard pursuers. Twice I could have sworn there was knocking at the door. At last, I fell asleep. When I awoke, the clocks were striking five. The candles were out. The wind raged in the darkness.

This is the end of the second stage of Pip's expectations.

| 10 |

The Past Links My Convict to Miss Havisham

In the morning, my dreaded visitor came out of his room. He had an even worse look by daylight.

"I have decided," said I, "to tell people that you are my uncle."

"Yes, dear boy! You can call me Uncle Provis. My real name is Magwitch—Abel Magwitch. I took the name of Provis on the ship to England."

"Were you tried in London?"

He nodded. "First knowed Mr. Jaggers that way. He was my lawyer."

After breakfast, I set out for Jaggers'. I had to be sure the story I'd heard was true.

"Sir, I have been informed by a person named Abel Magwitch that he is my benefactor," said I.

"That is the man," said Mr. Jaggers.

"I had always supposed it was Miss Havisham. It looked so like it."

"Take nothing on its looks, Mr. Pip. There's no better rule."

The next morning, I bought clothes for Magwitch. But it was hopeless to try to disguise him. He dragged his leg as if there were still an iron on it. I had to think of a way to get him safely out of England.

One night, there came a welcome footstep on the stairs. Magwitch, who had been asleep, jumped at the noise. I saw an open jackknife in his hand.

"It's Herbert!" I said quickly.

"Pip, dear fellow," cried Herbert, "how are you? I have been away for so long that I ...Hello! I beg your pardon!" Herbert saw Magwitch who now held out a black book.

"Swear on the good book," he said to Herbert. "Swear you shall never repeat what you hear!"

"Do as he wishes," I said.

Once satisfied with Herbert's oath, Magwitch began his tale. "Dear boy and Pip's comrade, I am going to tell you my life like a story. I'll make short work of the early part. I was a ragged little creature what never knew his parents. In jail and out of jail—that's how I grew up.

"More than 20 years ago," he went on, "I met a man I'd kill if I saw today. His name was Compeyson." Magwitch looked at me. "That's the man, dear boy, that you saw me a-pounding in the ditch. This Compeyson seemed like a gentleman. He had smooth talk and was good-looking, too.

"Compeyson had a friend called Arthur. They had been in a bad thing with a rich lady some years before. Her own brother put us on to her. They'd made a pot of money by it, too. Then Arthur got sick and had a vision. He called out, 'She's here with me. I can't get rid of her. She's all in white, with white flowers in her hair. She's coming for me.' Then he up and died.

"Compeyson seemed glad to be rid of Arthur. Him and me planned all sorts of things. He had me under his thumb. My wife had a hard time with it. But, stop . . . I won't bring her into this tale.

"In the end, me and Compeyson got caught with stolen money. Compeyson came to court looking like a gentleman. I looked miserably poor. Well, didn't Compeyson's lawyer blame it all on me? Didn't he point out how Compeyson was so well brought up? And wasn't Compeyson given just seven years and me fourteen?

"We were put on the same prison ship. When I learned that Compeyson had escaped to those marshes, too, I hunted him down. I smashed his face. I'd have killed him if they hadn't captured us."

"Is he dead now?" I asked.

Magwitch shook his head. "I can't say. I never heard no more of him."

Herbert pushed a note toward me. As Magwitch sat looking at the fire, I read it.

Miss Havisham's brother's name was Arthur. Compeyson is the man who pretended to be Miss Havisham's lover.

"Oh, what am I to do?" said I when Magwitch had gone to bed. "He is set on making me ever more the gentleman. He must be stopped!"

"You mean you can't accept…"

"How can I?" I broke in. "Look at him! I must never take another penny from him! But I am deeply in debt and now have *no* expectations. I have no calling. I am fit for nothing!"

"You can work with me!" Herbert said. My friend had no idea whose money had set up his business.

"The first thing is to get Magwitch out of England," Herbert said. "But I'm afraid he will not go without you. You will have to go along with him."

We sat in silence. Then I told Herbert I must leave him in charge of Magwitch for a while. I could not go abroad without first seeing Estella and Miss Havisham.

I found Estella alone with Miss Havisham. "I have learned who my benefactor is," said I to Miss Havisham. "It is not a fortunate discovery and must be my secret. Long ago, I fell into the mistake of thinking it was *you* who helped me. You led me on. Was that kind?"

Miss Havisham struck her stick upon the floor. "Foolish boy!" she cried. "Who am I that

I should be kind?"

"Miss Havisham, there are others you have hurt. You deeply wronged both Mr. Matthew Pocket and his son Herbert."

"What do you want for them?"

I said that Herbert had become my friend and that I had secretly set him up in business. I explained that for private reasons I could not continue to help him.

Then I turned to Estella. "You know that I have loved you since I first saw you. I thought Miss Havisham meant us for each other. I know now that is not true. Still, I must confess that I love you."

Estella turned to me. "You would not be warned, although I tried. Why not tell you the truth now? I am going to be married to Bentley Drummle."

"*Estella!* Put me aside if you must. But please give yourself to someone better than Drummle."

"I *am* going to be married to him," she said in a gentler voice. "You will get me out of your thoughts in a week."

"Never! You are a part of me! Oh, God

bless you. God forgive you!" I held her hand to my lips.

It was later that night, at the Blue Boar Inn, that I received a note from Miss Havisham. She asked me to come again.

I found her in the room across the landing. "I want to show you that I am not made of stone, Pip. There is something human in my heart," she said. "As to Herbert Pocket, I will give him the money he needs. But you must keep it a secret."

"Thank you, Miss Havisham."

To my amazement, she dropped down on her knees. "Oh, what have I done?" she cried. "It was *my* teachings that stole Estella's heart and put ice in its place!"

"I should have loved her anyway," I said gently.

"Pray forgive me," Miss Havisham cried. "—even if it is years from now and my broken heart has turned to dust!"

There was little more to say. I went down to the gate. Then suddenly I felt a sense of disaster. I rushed back to make sure that Miss Havisham was safe. I saw her seated by the hearth. As I turned to go, a great flame leaped up from the fire. Then Miss Havisham came running at me, shrieking. A whirl of fire blazed about her.

I threw my coat over her and smothered the flames. When help came at last, I found that my own hands were burned.

The doctor ordered Miss Havisham put to bed. She lay half awake, wandering in her speech. "What have I done?" she cried.

There was no more that I could do. Before I left her, I touched her lips with mine and whispered, "I forgive you."

Back at the Blue Boar a note waited for me. It contained three words in Wemmick's handwriting: *Don't go home.*

| 11 |

The Escape

I returned to London and went straight to Wemmick's house. He told me that my chambers had been watched by a suspicious looking stranger.

Wemmick had clearly been thinking about my problems. "I understand," he said, "that Herbert's friend Clara lives near the river. Should somebody want to slip on board a boat—well, if he stayed there, he would be ready to leave quickly."

Magwitch was soon made comfortable in Clara's house by the river. When the time was right, Herbert and I planned to row Magwitch out to some foreign steamship. I would board with him. Together we would sail out of the country.

The days passed. Though my burns healed slowly, I was soon well enough to dine with

Mr. Jaggers. He told me that Miss Havisham had been true to her word. She had written a check to Herbert's account. The money would let Herbert open his own firm in the East. This was the only good thing I had completed since I was first told of my great expectations.

Jaggers' housekeeper Molly served our meal. I looked at her closely. Her eyes were Estella's eyes. Now I felt certain that this must be Estella's mother!

Later, I shared my belief with Wemmick. He told me that Molly had once been arrested for murder. Jaggers had been her lawyer. Molly had one child—a little girl. It was said that, in a fit of anger, she killed the child. But that had never been proven.

When Herbert changed my bandages, we talked of Magwitch and his escape.

"I sat with him while you were away, Pip," Herbert said. "He told me more of his life. It seems he had a jealous wife who was once tried for murder. Mr. Jaggers got her off. Magwitch and his wife had a daughter." Herbert paused. "And now comes the dark part of the tale. He says that, in a jealous rage, the woman killed their child!"

"Herbert, did he tell you when this happened?"

"How old were you when you met him in the churchyard?"

"I think in my seventh year."

"It happened some three or four years before that. He says you reminded him of the little girl he had lost. She would have been about your age."

"Herbert," said I, "the man we have hiding down by the river is Estella's father!"

"We will need Startop," Herbert said. "He and I shall row, and you can steer. Magwitch need only sit quietly."

The plan was set. But before it could be carried out, I found a letter in the box. It said this:

Come to the marshes tonight at nine. If you want information about your "Uncle Provis," meet me at the little water shed. Tell no one. Come alone.

I caught the next coach and went straight to the water shed on the marshes.

A small candle glowed in the dark shed.

"Now," a voice growled, "I've got you!"

My arms were pulled close to my side. My burned arm screamed in pain. I struggled until I was tied tight to the wall.

Feeling faint and sick, I saw my attacker move into the candlelight. The flame of light showed me Orlick.

"Why have you set upon me in the dark?" I asked.

"Because you are my enemy. You gave me a bad name. You was in old Orlick's way ever since you was a child. Now, I'm a-going to have your life! I'm going to do to you what I did to your sister."

He held the candle close to my face.

"The burned child dreads the fire!" he laughed. "Old Orlick knows you are a-smuggling your Uncle Provis away. I know there's him that wants Magwitch."

Then I saw him raise a stone hammer. I shouted with all my might. At almost the same instant, I heard answering shouts and saw shapes in the door. I saw Orlick struggle with two men, leap quickly over the table, and fly out into the dark of night!

Next thing I knew, Herbert and Startop were bending over me. "Gently, Pip," said Herbert. "Can you stand?"

"Yes, yes. I can walk."

Herbert told me that I had dropped my letter from Orlick. He had found it and come after me. Now we gave up all thoughts of chasing Orlick. We had to get Magwitch away!

We chose one of those March days when the sun shines hot and the wind blows cold. We had our thick coats, and I took a bag. Where I might go or when I might return were questions unknown to me. My mind was wholly set on Magwitch's safety.

Herbert, Startop, and I rowed out on the River Thames. I looked toward the spot where Magwitch would meet us.

"I see him, Herbert!" I cried, pointing to shore.

Magwitch had on a dark cloak and carried a black bag.

"Dear boy!" he said as he took his seat. "Well done." He seemed to be the least nervous of any of us.

"If all goes well," said I, "you will be safe

within a few hours."

It was half past one when we saw the steamship's smoke. We said a tearful goodbye to Herbert and Startop.

Just then a four-oared galley shot out from the bank ahead. It fell alongside us. One of the men in the boat sat wrapped in a cloak, much like the one Magwitch wore.

The steamer was nearing us fast. The beating of her paddles grew louder.

"You have a convict," shouted a rower in the galley. "That's him, wrapped in the cloak. His name is Abel Magwitch, also called Provis. I'm here to arrest that man."

As the galley pulled up, the man grabbed Magwitch's shoulder. At the same time, Magwitch reached out to the cloaked man and pulled down his hood. I saw the face clearly—it was the other convict of long ago! I knew now that it must be Compeyson! Then I heard a great cry on board the steamer and a loud splash. I felt the boat sink from under me.

For only an instant I struggled. Then I was taken on the galley. Herbert was there. Startop was there. But our boat was gone, and the two convicts were gone. We looked at the water. Soon, a dark object bobbed up. As it floated nearer, I saw that it was Magwitch! He was quickly taken on board and chained at the wrists and ankles.

The men on the steamer did not seem to realize what had happened. It drifted away. A lookout was kept for the other convict, but at length we gave it up.

As we pulled for shore, Magwitch told me he was hurt. His chest had been injured, and he had a deep cut in his head. He did not know what he had done to Compeyson. He said that they had struggled fiercely underwater and then separated.

Being too ill for the prison, Magwitch was placed in the infirmary. I was at his side whenever they allowed it. I felt that was my place. All the distaste I had felt toward him melted away. Now I only saw a grateful man who had meant to be my benefactor. In truth, I was looking at a much better man than I had been to Joe.

| 12 |

Final Partings and New Beginnings

Each time I visited Magwitch, his breathing seemed more painful. I told him how sorry I was to think he had come back to England for my sake.

"I'm quite content," he answered. "I've seen my boy, and he can be a gentleman without me."

But I knew his hopes would not come true. He was a criminal. The state would take everything he owned.

Magwitch became weaker each day. One evening, as I entered the room, he seemed changed—more peaceful somehow. He smiled at me, and I laid my hand on his breast. He put both his hands upon it.

"Dear Magwitch," I said, "I must tell you something. I know that you had a child once,

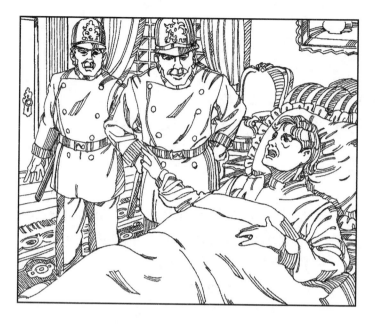

a girl you loved and lost."

I felt him press on my hand.

"I want you to know that she lived and found powerful friends. She is a lady now and very beautiful. And I love her!"

He raised my hand to his lips. Then he looked up at the ceiling, and passed away.

"O Lord," I prayed, "be merciful to him, a sinner!"

Magwitch was gone. Herbert had set up his business in the East. I was alone and in debt. With Magwitch gone, there was no income.

And, I was very ill. For days I lay on the sofa with a high fever. I had no purpose.

Then one morning I awoke to find two men standing by my bed.

"You are arrested, sir," said one. "You are to be taken to debtors' prison."

I tried to get up, but could not. "I would come with you if I could," I said, "but I am quite unable. If you take me from here, I think I shall die."

They must have left me. I remember little of the next days. But one night, there in the chair at my bedside, sat Joe.

"Oh, Joe. You break my heart!" I cried. "Please look angry at me, Joe. Tell me I was ungrateful. You must not be kind to me!"

"Oh, no, dear Pip," said Joe, "you and me was ever friends." I held his dear, rough hand, and we both felt happy.

Joe took care of me until I was strong again. He told me about all that had changed on the marshes. Not only had Biddy taught him to read, she had also become his wife! Miss Havisham had died, leaving most of her fortune to Estella. She had also left a share of money to Mr. Matthew Pocket. As for Orlick, he had been caught robbing Pumblechook's office and was in jail.

As I grew stronger, Joe became less easy with me. He began calling me "sir" again. One morning I woke to find this note:

You are well again, dear Pip, and will do better without me.

—Jo

P.S. Ever the best of friends.

Along with the letter was a receipt. It showed that Joe had paid my debts.

I followed him to the forge to beg his forgiveness and friendship. I thanked Joe and Biddy for all they'd done for me. Still, knowing that Estella had married Drummle was too much for me. So I sold what I had and joined Herbert in the East. I became a clerk—and, after many a year, a partner in the firm. I lived fairly happily with Herbert and Clara. I wrote often to Biddy and Joe.

In time, Herbert learned of my part in his business affairs. He was much amazed and moved. It's true that our firm never made great sums of money, but we worked hard and had a good name.

It was 11 years later when I next laid my hand on the old kitchen door. There by the fire sat Joe. And there, on his own little stool, was Joe and Biddy's son.

"We gave him the name of Pip," said Joe. "Both of us hoped he might grow to be a little bit like you."

At dinner, Joe told me that Estella's husband had treated her badly. Only recently the shameful brute had died in an accident.

I wanted to revisit Miss Havisham's house and think of Estella once more. The big house was gone. Only a wall of the weedy garden remained. There, coming toward me, was a lonely figure.

"Estella!" I cried out.

"I am greatly changed," she said. "I wonder you know me. The years have been hard, Pip. Yet suffering has given me a heart! It has taught me to understand what *your* heart used to feel. Tell me we are friends."

"We are friends," I said.

"And we will continue friends," said Estella.

I took her hand in mine. Together we went

out of the ruined place. The evening mists were rising. In the peaceful light, I saw no shadow of another parting from her.

Activities
Great Expectations

BOOK SEQUENCE

First complete the sentences with words from the box. Then number the events to show which happened first, second, and so on. You will not use all the words in the box.

wrench	engaged	pile	handcuffs	introduced
swore	hammer	lie	receipt	blacksmith
gravy	merciful	stole	pudding	rewarding
adopted	affairs	file	money	appearances

_____ 1. Herbert told Pip that Miss Havisham had _____ Estella.

_____ 2. Orlick came at Pip with a stone _____.

_____ 3. Pip _____ a beautiful pork pie.

_____ 4. Estella told Pip that she was _____ to Drummle.

_____ 5. On Christmas Eve, Pip's job was to stir the _____.

_____ 6. At Miss Havisham's, Pip _____ himself as "Pumblechook's boy."

_____ 7. The convict apologized to the _____ for stealing his food.

_____ 8. Herbert _____ he would not repeat what Magwitch told him.

_____ 9. A soldier asked Joe to mend some _____.

_____ 10. A _____ showed that Joe had paid Pip's debts.

_____ 11. Joe told Pip not to _____ to him again.

_____ 12. Pip prayed that God would be _____ to Magwitch.

_____ 13. The prisoner rasped a _____ against his leg iron.

_____ 14. Jaggers told Pip to take his _____ into his own hands.

81

FACTS ABOUT CHARACTERS
Reread Chapter 1 and answer below.

A. Write a letter to match each character on the left with his or her description on the right.

1. ___ **Pip**   a. black hair and eyes; tall and bony

2. ___ **the convict**   b. a sad bundle of shivers

3. ___ **Joe Gargery**   c. frightening; dressed in rough gray clothes

4. ___ **Mrs. Joe**   d. good-natured; blond hair, blue eyes

B. Who said what? Write a character's name next to each line of dialogue.

1. _____: "Don't say a word about me or your heart and your liver shall be roasted and ate!"

2. _____: "Where have you been, you monkey?"

3. _____: "He was dressed like you, only with a hat."

4. _____: "Get behind the door, old chap."

C. Circle two words that describe each character.

1. **Pip**   orphan   impatient   young   brutal

2. **Joe Gargery**   elderly   sympathetic   blacksmith   convict

3. **the convict**   hungry   innocent   grateful   stylish

4. **Mrs. Joe**   good-natured   strict   lean   beautiful

SYNONYMS AND ANTONYMS

Reread Chapter 5 and then answer below.

A. Find a (word that means the same) in the box for each **boldface** word and write it on the line. You will not use all the words in the box.

occupation	furious	dissatisfied	admired	evil
delighted	invited	disagreeable	gloomy	hobby

1. Mr. Joe was **angry** _____ that she had not been **asked** _____ to visit Miss Havisham.

2. Mrs. Joe was **thrilled** _____ with the 25 pounds.

3. Orlick was a **sour** _____, **moody** _____ fellow.

4. Miss Havisham's words had a **wicked** _____ ring.

5. Pip became **unhappy** _____ with his **trade** _____ and his life.

B. Find a (word that means the opposite) in the box for each **boldface** word. Write the antonym on the line. You will not use all the words in the box.

disturbed	sorry	object	unqualified
disliked	faint	promise	unrewarded

1. Pip **enjoyed** _____ the family's dinner at the inn.

2. A **heavy** _____ mist hung in the air as Pip headed home.

83

3. Jaggers asked Pip to **agree** _____
   to two things.

4. Pip was to be placed under a
   proper _____ tutor.

5. Biddy and Joe said they were
   glad _____ for Pip, but
   there was sadness in their voices.

CAUSE AND EFFECT
Reread Chapter 7 and answer below.

A. Read the on the left. Then write a letter to show the
of each .

CAUSE

1. ___ Biddy wrote that
   Joe was coming
   to London.

2. ___ Pip saw that Estella
   had grown into an
   elegant lady.

3. ___ Matthew Pocket's
   teaching earned
   him little money.

4. ___ Being with Joe now
   made Pip feel guilty
   and uncomfortable.

5. ___ Dressed up in city
   clothes, Joe felt silly.

6. ___ Drummle was
   flattered by Mr.
   Jaggers' attentions.

EFFECT

a. He felt like a
   coarse, common
   boy again.

b. He went home
   instead of staying
   for dinner.

c. Pip was not happy
   to hear the news.

d. He walked on the
   other side of the
   street from his
   friend.

e. He rented rooms
   to his students.

f. He stayed the
   night at the
   Blue Boar Inn.

B. Write **T** if the statement is or **F** if the statement is.

1. ___ Mr. Jaggers' tight grip on Molly's arm was the of her scar.

2. ___ Pip's feeling of anger was the of hearing Joe call him "sir."

3. ___ Joe's message from Miss Havisham was the of Pip's face turning red.

4. ___ Orlick's presence at Miss Havisham's was the of Pip's surprise.

COMPREHENSION CHECK

Reread Chapter 9. Then circle a letter to show how each sentence should be completed.

1. Pip was 23 years old when
   a. his parents died.   b. Magwitch came to visit.

2. Magwitch looked around Pip's room as if
   a. he had some part   b. he'd like to steal
   in what he saw.   Pip's fine things.

3. Pip didn't recognize Magwitch until
   a. he pulled off his hat   b. he tied a handkerchief
   and showed his face.   around his head.

4. Magwitch's eyes filled with tears when
   a. Pip said they   b. he remembered
   could not be   the day they met in
   friends.   the churchyard.

5. Magwitch said he had lived a hard life
   a. because his income   b. so that Pip could
   had been so small.   live an easy one.

6. Only Magwitch and Mr. Jaggers had known that

    a. Magwitch was   b. Miss Havisham was
       Pip's benefactor.   Pip's benefactor.

7. Magwitch had made his fortune

    a. in England.   b. in Australia.

8. Pip wondered if Magwitch's hand was

    a. stained with blood.   b. badly injured.

FINAL EXAM

A. Circle a letter to correctly answer each question or complete each statement.

1. What two names were combined to make the name Pip?

    a. Peter and Gargery   c. Philip and Pirrip

    b. Paul and Pirrip   d. Patrick and Phipps

2. Why was the prisoner happy to hear that Pip lived with a blacksmith?

    a. He needed a forge.   c. His horse lost a shoe.

    b. He needed a file.   d. His handcuffs were broken.

3. The two things Estella criticized about Pip were

    a. his coarse shoes   c. his coarse hands
       and thick hands.   and thick boots.

    b. his lack of manners.   d. his lack of money

4. At first, who did Pip think was his benefactor?

    a. Mr. Jaggers   c. Miss Havisham

    b. Matthew Pocket   d. Abel Magwitch

5. The first lesson that Herbert taught Pip was

    a. not to eat with a knife.

    c. to always wear expensive clothes.

    b. to say please and thank you.

    d. not to be deceived by appearances.

B. Answer each question in your own words. Write in complete sentences.

1. Describe the way Miss Havisham lived. Why had she chosen to live that way?

_____

_____

_____

_____

2. Estella said that Miss Havisham had taught her "not to have a heart." What did she mean by that?

_____

_____

_____

_____

3. Name at least two ways that Biddy made Joe a happier man.

_____

_____

_____

_____

Answers to Activities
Great Expectations

BOOK SEQUENCE
1. 8/adopted   2. 12/hammer   3. 2/stole   4. 11/engaged
5. 1/pudding   6. 6/introduced   7. 5/blacksmith
8. 10/swore   9. 4/handcuffs   10. 13/receipt
11. 7/lie   12. 14/merciful   13. 3/file   14. 9/affairs

FACTS ABOUT CHARACTERS
A. 1. b   2. c   3. d   4. a
B. 1. the convict   2. Mrs. Joe   3. Pip   4. Joe
C. 1. orphan, young   2. sympathetic, blacksmith
    3. hungry, grateful   4. strict, lean

SYNONYMS AND ANTONYMS
A. 1. furious, invited   2. delighted   3. disagreeable, gloomy
    4. evil   5. dissatisfied, occupation
B. 1. disliked   2. faint   3. object   4. unqualified   5. sorry

CAUSE AND EFFECT
A. 1. c   2. a   3. e   4. f   5. b   6. d
B. 1. F   2. T   3. F   4. T

COMPREHENSION CHECK
1. b   2. a   3. b   4. a   5. b   6. a   7. b   8. a

FINAL EXAM
A. 1. c   2. b   3. c   4. c   5. a
B. Answers will vary but should approximate:
    1. She lived in the past. Because her lover hadn't
        married her, she left her wedding preparations
        in place and lived in their presence.
    2. Miss Havisham taught her to feel no tenderness
        or softness. She wanted Estella to be heartless
        in her dealings with the men who loved her.
    3. She taught him to read. She married him.
        She gave him a son.